Ariel's Secret

By Melissa Lagonegro

Illustrated by Atelier Philippe Harchy

Random House 🏠 New York

Copyright © 2005 Disney Enterprises, Inc. All rights reserved under International and Pan-American Copyright Conventions. Published in the United States by Random House Children's Books, a division of Random House, Inc., New York, NY 10019, and simultaneously in Canada by Random House of Canada Limited, Toronto, in conjunction with Disney Enterprises, Inc. RANDOM HOUSE and colophon are registered trademarks of Random House, Inc.

Library of Congress Control Number: 2004093749   ISBN: 0-7364-2324-9

www.randomhouse.com/kids/disney

MANUFACTURED IN CHINA

10 9 8 7 6 5 4 3 2

Do you have a secret that you've never told anyone? I do—and I'm going to share it with you. My name is Ariel, and I used to keep a secret grotto where I collected things from the human world. I kept my special spot hidden for a long time, but eventually, my father discovered it.

But I have another secret—a secret that
even my best friend, Flounder, doesn't know.
When I was a little mermaid, I always
imagined what it was like on land, but my
father forbade me to go there.

One day, I disobeyed him and swam to the surface. I was a bit nervous about what I'd find, but I was so excited to see land for the very first time.

I watched birds fly and felt the warm sun
beat down on my face. But something else
happened when I reached land—something
I've kept secret for a long, long time . . . a
human saw me!

I saw him first. He was a young boy with dark hair and blue eyes. I watched him from a distance as he splashed around in the water with a furry little animal he called Max.

The boy seemed kind, gentle, and very funny.
But his furry friend heard me giggling and
started to make a loud woofing noise.

I tried to hide behind a rock, but it was too
late. The boy saw me and my tail.

At first, I was scared. I had always been told that humans were dangerous. What if he told other humans that he had seen me? They might come after the merfolk and destroy our world.

I was about to dive back into the sea when I
heard a voice. "Don't go," said the boy. "I won't
hurt you." He smiled and ran toward me.

As the boy came closer, he gently stretched
out his hand, and something in his eyes told
me that I wasn't in danger.

Our meeting was quickly cut short.

"Dinnertime," called a voice from the distance.

"Hurry, dive back into the sea," said the boy.

"You can't be seen. I promise to keep you a secret."

We smiled at each other, and I knew he
would never tell anyone that we'd met.
It was our little secret, and I trusted him.

Time passed, and I continued to go to the surface to collect items from the humans. I dreamed that someday I would be a part of their world, but I never saw that boy again.

Years later, while exploring, I noticed the shadow of a ship sailing overhead. I swam to the surface to get a better look, and that's when I saw the handsome young man.

The other humans called him Prince Eric.
I didn't recognize him at first, but I had a
strange feeling that I'd seen him before.

Suddenly, the winds whipped and huge
waves crashed into the boat. The ship was
caught in a hurricane! Prince Eric fell into the
ocean, and it was up to me to save him.

I used all my strength to rescue Eric and
return him safely to shore. As I stared at his
handsome face, I knew for sure that he was
the boy I'd met years ago.

When I returned to the sea, my father
found out I had been to the surface. He
was furious! I wanted to tell Flounder
I had met the prince before, but I
couldn't. If my secret got out, my father
would be even angrier.

I had to see the prince again, and
although it wasn't easy, I made my way
to the shore—this time on legs.

Eric and I spent more time
together, and I knew he was the man I
wanted to be with forever.

After an unbelievable adventure,
we were married. As we sailed away
as husband and wife, I knew that Eric
and I were destined to be together.

One day I will tell Eric everything, but for now I like keeping it my own little secret. It makes my love for Eric even more special. Thanks for letting me share my secret with you!